There's a UNICORN IN YOUR BOOK

Written by TOM FLETCHER

Illustrated by GREG ABBOTT

PUFFIN

For Buzz, Buddy and Max – T.F.

For Anikka – G.A.

PUFFIN BOOKS

UK | USA | Canada | Ireland | Australia | India | New Zealand | South Africa

Puffin Books is part of the Penguin Random House group of companies whose addresses can be found at global.penguinrandomhouse.com.

www.penguin.co.uk
www.puffin.co.uk
www.ladybird.co.uk

Penguin
Random House
UK

First published 2021

001

Copyright © Tom Fletcher, 2021
Illustrated by Greg Abbott

The moral right of the author has been asserted

Printed in China

The authorized representative in the EEA is Penguin Random House Ireland, Morrison Chambers, 32 Nassau Street, Dublin D02 YH68

A CIP catalogue record for this book is available from the British Library

ISBN: 978-0-241-46660-5

All correspondence to:
Puffin Books, Penguin Random House Children's
One Embassy Gardens, 8 Viaduct Gardens, London SW11 7BW

GALLOPING GLITTER!
There's a **UNICORN** in your book!

I bet the next page will be full of
songs about rainbows and sparkles –
unicorns love to **SING**...

Hmmm . . . this unicorn isn't singing.
What's wrong, Unicorn?

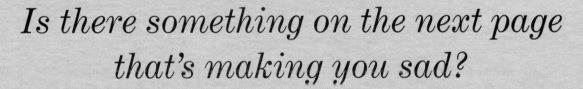

*Is there something on the next page
that's making you sad?*

Shall we have a look and see?

UH-OH! It's a worry gremlin!

No wonder Unicorn isn't singing –
you don't want a worry gremlin in your book.

Wiggle your fingers to make some
magic dust – that should help.

WOW!

Now there's magic dust everywhere.
(And even
a few
fairies!)

Did it work?
Has the
worry gremlin gone?

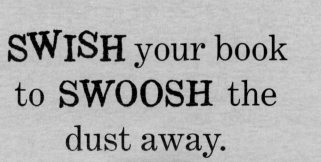

SWISH your book
to **SWOOSH** the
dust away.

The worry gremlin is gone! But . . .
Unicorn still isn't singing.

I know!
Unicorns *love* to be tickled under the chin ...
Let's try some **TICKLING!**

Oh dear. This unicorn does NOT like tickling.
We should have asked first.

Sorry, Unicorn!

Let's try to make Unicorn smile –
tell your **FUNNIEST JOKE**.

What do you call a
unicorn with a cold?

Well . . . *that* didn't work at all.

And wait – what are those holes in your book?

Oh no! **MORE** worry gremlins!
They seem to enjoy Unicorn worrying.

How mean!

Try giving your book a **SHAKE** –

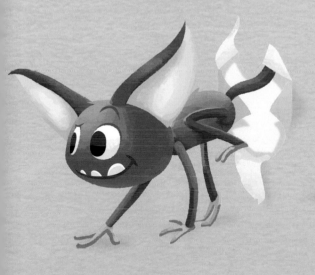

that might get rid of them.

OOOOPS!

Now Unicorn's horn is stuck in the page!

Give your book another
gentle **SHAKE** – *really gently . . .*

Well done – Unicorn is free!

Now it's time to get rid of these
worry gremlins once and for all.

I KNOW!

The best way to get rid of a worry
is to tell someone about it.

And I think there might be someone
on the next page who can help us . . .

It's Unicorn's friend, Monster!
That's perfect!

Unicorn, whisper your worry to Monster
and you'll definitely feel better!

HURRAH! Unicorn is much happier now.
The worry gremlins have started to fade . . .

Maybe *you* could try
whispering something too?

Hold the book very close
and whisper in Unicorn's ear.

Shhh . . .
whisper *really quietly* . . .

It looks as though whatever you whispered
has worked! Now Unicorn feels better
and is ready to sing . . .

Shall we join in?

Clear your throat, sit up straight,
and let's count everyone in.

1...2...3...4...

Rainbow sparkle, rainbow sparkle,
Shine across the sky!
Makes me happy, makes me happy,
Nobody knows why!

Well done, Unicorn!
Well done, Monster!

And well done, you!

The worry gremlins
are gone from your book for good.

I think it's time to celebrate with . . .

A UNICORN PARTY! Woohoo!
Can we give you a hug, Unicorn?

YES!

Then let's give your book a big hug goodbye.